LIFE OF DODGE CITY

PART 1

Cody Pattan

Life of Dodge City — Part 1
By Cody Pattan

First Edition eBook: 2018
First Edition Paperback: 2018

ISBN (ePub): 978-0-9997078-0-7
ISBN (Paperback): 978-0-9997078-1-4

Cover Copyright © 2018 Cody Pattan
Cover design by Isaiah Silkwood
Formatting by Polgarus Studio

Published in the United States of America

To my Aunt Dot, I think she's a really great Auntie.

Prologue

Once upon a time, in the old west, there lived a sheriff named Joe Luke. He was the fastest gunman in the west.

He did some farming in Montana and also owned a gold mine in Montana that people tried to steal from him.

He sold that gold mine to Billy Bob, Blondy, Steve, and Brindy Pattan.

Billy Bob and Blondy, their dad Steve and their mom Brindy, were friends with Joe Luke, and they live in Dodge City.

Chapter 1

Joe Luke, Blondy, Billy Bob, Steve, and Brindy saw these two guys fighting over a woman in a saloon.

Bill Smith Sr. shoved Frank Cooper Sr. on the left shoulder. Frank responded by punching Bill Smith Sr. in the face.

Joe Luke stepped in between them both and spread them apart with his arms, saying in an ornery voice, "Now you two knock it off."

Bill Smith Sr. backed up and Frank Cooper Sr. slugged Joe Luke in the face giving him a black eye. Joe Luke went down to the ground. He got back up and jabbed Frank Cooper Sr. in the face and the stomach, sending Frank stumbling back in pain.

The sheriff took Frank Cooper Sr. to jail for a year.

~·~·~

Right after the sheriff put Frank Cooper Sr. in jail, he went to the saloon to have a beer with Doc Smith and Deputy Morgan.

The sheriff, Deputy Morgan, Doc and a few other people heard a gunshot from out of nowhere.

They went into the ally next to the Long Branch Saloon where they saw a person lying on the ground.

Sheriff Joe Luke knelt down next to the body. "Darreled Pattan has been shot in the back."

Hank Jones, a cow hand on a cattle drive, brushed his salt and pepper hair back. "Why would somebody kill Darreled Pattan?"

Joe Luke stood up and turned his head to Deputy Morgan. "I am going to find out who killed Darreled. Will you please look after things here in Dodge City?"

Deputy Morgan smiled. "I won't let you down."

Joe Luke smiled back. "Okay, I hope you don't let me down."

"Thank you sheriff, you can count on me."

Joe Luke bent over and picked up the body. He took Darreled to the Dodge City cemetery with the men and had a big funeral.

~·~·~

Joe Luke heard a train whistle. "The train is coming."

Mac Jenkins Sr. adjusted his gun belt and brushed off his pants. "Can some of you men help me unload my stuff at the hardware store?"

Bill Smith Sr. smiled. "Yes Sir."

Mac Jenkins Sr. pointed at the train station hitching post and his hardware store. "Okay men, let's load these mules and take them to my hardware store."

Mac Jenkins Sr. and the men took his supplies that the mules were carrying on their backs.

The train left Dodge City to get some money from the bank in Hays City and more supplies.

Then Sheriff Joe Luke went out of town for a while.

Chapter 2

Deputy Morgan saw two men in the street preparing for a shootout.

He hunched over and put his right hand on the six gun in his holster. "You two guys in the street. What are you doing this shooting for?

Bob Peck replied to the Deputy, "Billy Peck Sr. is trying to take my woman from me."

Billy's face was white with fear. "You're lying, Bob."

"No, I am not lying to you, Billy." Bob replied.

Julie Peck called out from the side of the street, "You're lying, Billy Peck Sr."

Deputy Morgan turned to Billy. "I am trying to keep you out of trouble."

Billy Peck Sr. sighed with relief. "Thank you for trying to keep me out of trouble. Can you put me in jail? Away from him."

"Sure I can." Deputy Morgan pointed his finger at Billy. "Okay, Billy, let's go to jail then."

Billy Peck Sr. cuffed his hands. "Okay, sounds good to me then."

Billy Peck Sr. waved his right hand at Bob Peck. "Goodbye, Bob."

Bob started walking next to them and pointed his finger at Billy. "I may never see you ever again, Billy."

Billy pointed back. "I hope I don't see you anymore."

"If you come near my woman, I will shoot you in the back three times right here in the street." Bob pointed at Billy Peck Sr.

Billy Peck Sr. pointed his finger back at Bob as they entered the sheriff's office. "We will see about that, Bob."

Bob Peck was mad. "You know I will gun you down here in Dodge City."

Deputy Morgan pushed Billy Peck Sr. into the jail cell, shut the door, and pointed his finger at both of them. "There will be no gunfight in Dodge City."

Bob pointed his finger at Deputy Morgan. "Yes there will be a gunfight here in Dodge City."

Deputy Morgan yelled at Bob Peck. "If you are having a gunfight, go do it up in the hills already."

Bob Peck put both hands on his gun belt. "I will deal with him later if I have to."

Deputy Morgan replied. "Okay that will be better then."

Bob Peck and Deputy Morgan walked out of the office and Bob pointed his finger at the deputy's face. "I will go up to the hills to have a gunfight then. Tell Bill that I will see him up there later today."

Deputy Morgan nodded his head. "Okay I will, Bob. I will give Billy Peck Sr. the message right now then."

Bob pointed his finger and replied to Deputy Morgan, "Okay."

Deputy Morgan yelled, "Get out of town!"

Bob shook his left fist. "I hope you trip over that badge someday deputy and same with the sheriff.

Deputy Morgan reached for his gun and pointed at Bob Peck. "Get out now or else I am going to put a bullet in you."

Bob Peck clenched his fist. "Fine, Deputy, I will be back." He walked to the stable, saddled up his horse, and rode out of town.

For now.

~ ~ ~

Deputy Morgan went back to the jail where Billy Peck Sr. waited.

Billy Peck Sr. said to the deputy, "What did Bob say to you, my friend?"

Deputy Morgan walked into the sheriff's office where Billy Peck Sr. was and talked to him from outside of the cell door. "He is going to meet you up in the hills now. Okay, I am letting you out, Billy Peck Sr."

Deputy Morgan grabbed the keys, off the nail on the wall, with his left hand and sorted through them with his right hand. He put the key in the lock and turned it to the right, opening the cell door.

Billy Peck Sr. walked out of the cell door. "Okay thank you, Deputy Morgan."

Deputy Morgan gave Billy Peck Sr. a thumbs up. "You bet, Billy Peck Sr."

Billy Peck Sr. gave Deputy Morgan a thumbs up before he walked out of the sheriff's office door. "Wish me luck, Deputy Morgan."

Deputy Morgan looked at Billy Peck Sr. "I will wish you luck.

Billy looked at Deputy Morgan. "Well I better go up to the hills then."

Deputy Morgan shook Billy's right hand and gave him an awesome smile. "Okay."

Billy Peck Sr. looked at Deputy Morgan. "Bye, Deputy Morgan."

Deputy Morgan waved back at Billy Peck Sr. as he went out the door. "Bye."

~ ~ ~

Billy Peck Sr. dismounted his horse and looked around for Bob Peck.

Bob Peck came out from behind the bushes and shouted. "I am going to kill you for trying to steal my woman."

Billy Peck Sr. walked up close to Bob Peck with his hands out. "I was just buying your woman a drink, Bob."

Bob Peck yelled at him. "I had about enough of you."

Billy Peck Sr. yelled while moving his hands around. "No I had about enough of you, Bob."

Bob Peck stomped his left foot on the ground. "I hate you, Billy Peck Sr., for trying to steal my woman."

Billy Peck Sr. put both of his hands on his belt. "I was just being nice to your woman."

Bob Peck put both of his hands on his hips. "I had about enough of this conversation now draw that gun of yours."

Billy Peck Sr. put his right hand on his gun and hunched over, about to draw. He drew his gun and Bob Peck shot him twice.

Chapter 3

Mac Jenkins Sr. ran inside the jail. "Sheriff, Sheriff, are you there? Deputy, have you seen the sheriff anywhere?"

Deputy Morgan put both hands on his belt. "The Sheriff told me that he was heading to the saloon to have a beer why?"

"Hank Jones is in town."

"Where at?"

"He is at the Dodge House right now."

"Thank you for the update. I'll let the Sheriff know I'll keep an eye on him. Hank Jones always gets in trouble with different lawmen."

"You are welcome."

"See you later Mac Jenkins Sr.."

Mac Jenkins Sr. waved his right hand. "Bye."

Deputy Morgan grabbed his hat and headed for the saloon. "Thanks for stopping by, Mac Jenkins Sr.."

Mac Jenkins Sr. looked at Deputy Morgan. "No problem, Deputy Morgan. You are a good friend, Deputy."

～•～•～

Deputy Morgan ran though the saloon doors, while heading up to the bar. "Sheriff."

Joe Luke looked at Deputy Morgan. "Yes Deputy." The sheriff set his beer on the counter while the Deputy was talking.

"Mac Jenkins Sr. told me that Hank Jones is in town."

"Oh, that ruffian. Thank you for letting me know, Deputy Morgan."

"What are you going to do now, Sheriff Joe Luke?"

Joe Luke shrugged his shoulders back. "Nothing right now he has not caused any trouble yet, Deputy Morgan. I'll keep an eye on him but I can't do anything right now. Unless he does something like shoots somebody, here in Dodge.

"Okay. I will head back to the jail."

"Okay."

"Bye."

"Bye." Replied Joe Luke.

Deputy Morgan went out the saloon doors.

Mac Jenkins Sr. waved at the Deputy. "Hey."

Deputy Morgan saluted back. "Hey."

"Where are you going."

"I am going to the jail."

Mac Jenkins Sr. smiled. "May I come."

Deputy Morgan smiled back. "Sure."

~·~·~

Joe Luke, Deputy Morgan, Mac Jenkins Sr., and everybody else heard another gunshot in the alley next to the Long Branch Saloon. Everyone gathered around.

Joe Luke came up behind everybody. "What happened?"

Ben Smith Jr. looked at Joe Luke. "Somebody has been shot in the back, sir."

Joe Luke bent over and rolled the body over with his right hand. "I don't believe it, Ben Smith Jr."

Ben Smith Jr. looked at the ground. "What is it, Joe Luke.

Joe Luke looked up and spoke to Ben Smith Jr."I know this person. His name is Joe Reed?"

Ben Smith Jr. gasped. "Really now."

Joe Luke spoke back. "Yep, it is true."

Bob Peck snickered. "Oh look it's the black eyed dork." He laughed his head off.

Joe Luke yelled at him. "Don't say that, Bob Peck."

"Why not, Joe Luke?" he replied.

Joe Luke yelled. "Because I don't want to be called that."

Bob grinned. "I like to call you a black eyed dork, especially in Dodge City."

Joe Luke went up to Bob Peck and smacked him in the face.

Bob fell to the ground.

~·~·~

Hank Jones went in the alley next to Long Branch Saloon.

Hank Jones walked up to crowd. "Hey, Joe Luke."

Joe Luke looked at Hank Jones with a mean look on his face. "What do you want, loser?"

Hank Jones pushed Payton Jones in front of him. "Look who I got here."

Joe Luke looked down. "Payton Jones! I thought you were supposed to be in school."

Payton looked up at Joe Luke. "We have a school here in Dodge?"

Joe Luke spoke to Payton. "Yes we do."

Hank Jones told Joe Luke. "You are not taking my cousin, Payton, to school. You hear me, sheriff?"

Joe Luke crouched down and was about to draw his six gun. "Yes I am, Hank Jones. I am taking Payton Jones to school."

Hank Jones got mad. "For the last time, no, Joe Luke."

Joe Luke stared at Hank jones. "You are going to jail for the murder of Joe Reed and Darreled Pattan."

Hank Jones made a fist at Joe Luke. "I am not going to jail, Joe Luke. You can't make me go."

Joe Luke put his left hand out. "Give me your gun, Hank Jones."

Hank Jones put his right hand on his pistol. "No thank you, Joe Luke. I am good for now."

Joe Luke yelled at Hank Jones. "Give me that gun now."

Hank Jones yelled back. "Come on. Let's see how fast you can draw that gun of yours, Joe Luke."

Joe Luke lifted his eyebrow. "You do not want to do this, Hank Jones."

Hank Jones gave Joe Luke a mean look. "Draw now."

Joe Luke put his left hand out. "No don't."

Hank Jones pulled his gun out of his holster and shot Joe Luke in the right leg.

Bang.

Joe Luke put his left hand on his right leg and pulled his six gun out of his holster, shooting Hank Jones twice in the chest.

Bang. Bang.

Hank Jones dropped his six gun into the dust and hung on to his chest trying to stop it from bleeding.

Joe Luke and Hank Jones fell to the ground at the same time.

Joe Luke struggled to holster his six gun.

Chapter 4

Billy Bob waved his hand at Joe Luke, outside the Long Branch Saloon. "Hey, Sheriff Joe Luke."

Joe Luke saluted. "Hey, Billy Bob and Blondy Pattan."

Blondy spoke to Joe Luke, "What happened to you?"

Joe Luke spoke, "Oh you remember. I got into a fight with Frank Cooper Sr., he slugged me in the left eye, and Hank Jones also shot me in the right leg Blondy."

Billy Bob glared. "That's not good, Joe Luke. What have you been up to, Sheriff?"

Joe Luke smiled. "Just doing the law." He gave a thumbs up.

Billy Bob smiled back. "That's cool."

Joe Luke shrugged his shoulders. "Yep it is true."

"I see."

"Yep."

Billy Bob glared at Joe Luke. "What are you going to do now, Sheriff?"

"Probably go to the Dodge House, Billy Bob." He pointed his finger at the Dodge House.

Billy Bob made eye contact with Joe Luke. "Can we come with you, up to the Dodge House, Sheriff Joe Luke?"

Joe Luke shrugged both of his shoulders. "Sure why not."

Billy Bob looked at Joe Luke. "Okay sounds like a plan."

They went inside the Dodge House and went up to the counter.

Joe Luke spoke to Duke Owens, "How are you today, my friend?"

Duke Owens spoke back, "I am good what happened to you, my friend?"

Joe Luke leaned on the Counter. "I got in a fight with Frank Cooper Sr. The one that slugged me in the left eye. I fell to the ground, got up, and jabbed him in the stomach and that's how I got this black eye."

Duke Owens gasped. "Well that's not good, Joe Luke."

Joe Luke spoke again, "Hank Jones also shot me once in the right leg and now I am on crutches."

Duke Owens shrugged his shoulders. "Well I feel sorry for you, Joe Luke."

Joe Luke raised his right hand in the air. "Why thank you, Duke Owens."

Duke Owens smiled at Joe Luke. "You are welcome, Sheriff Joe Luke. What are you up to today?"

"Not much just doing the law right now."

Duke Owens glared at Joe Luke. "That's good I am glad you are having fun with the law."

"Yep." The sheriff smiled at Duke Owens. "Hey Duke Owens. This is Billy Bob and Blondy Pattan."

Duke Owens looked at Billy Bob and Blondy. "It's nice to meet you, Billy Bob and Blondy Pattan," he said while shaking their hands.

Billy Bob asked Duke Owens a question. "Where is your wife, Daisy Owens?"

Duke Owens spoke back, "She is in the kitchen washing the dishes with a scrubber, you guys."

Billy Bob and Blondy looked each other in the eye. "That sounds like fun, Duke Owens."

Duke Owens looked back at Billy Bob and Blondy. "I will make sure to tell Daisy Owens that you said that."

Billy Bob smiled. "Okay sounds like a plan." He then made eye contact with Joe Luke. "So sheriff."

Joe Luke made eye contact back to Billy Bob. "Ya."

Billy Bob put his right hand out. "Where does Jane Macornic work?"

Joe Luke smiled at Billy Bob. "She works at the Lady Gay Saloon, my friend."

Billy Bob gave Joe Luke a thumbs up. "Is she liking it so far, my friend?"

Joe Luke gave Billy Bob a thumbs up. "Yep."

Billy Bob put his two hands up. "That's good. I am glad she is liking it so far, sheriff."

Joe Luke put his two hands up in the air. "Yep." He shrugged his shoulders. "Well, I am glad you met Duke Owens."

Billy Bob smiled at Joe Luke. "Yes indeed, I am glad that Blondy Pattan and I met him. He seems to be a nice man, Sheriff."

Joe Luke smiled back. "Indeed he is. I guess I will head back to the jail, Billy Bob and Blondy Pattan."

Billy Bob gave Joe Luke a wink. "Okay."

Joe Luke winked. "I will see you around Billy Bob and Blondy Pattan," he said with a wave. He saluted his friends while heading back to the jail.

Billy Bob waved back at Joe Luke. "Okay. Love you, brother in the Lord. Yee-Haw."

Joe Luke looked back at Billy Bob. "Love you guys too and Yee-Haw to you to guys as well."

~·~·~

Ben Smith Jr. walked up to the Sheriff. "Hey, Joe Luke," he said with a wave.

Joe Luke turned his neck to the left. "Hey Ben Smith Jr. ," he said with a salute.

Ben Smith Jr. put both hands on his gun belt. "Where are you going, Joe Luke?"

Joe Luke put both of his hands on his gun belt. "I am heading to the Long Branch Saloon to see Doc Smith."

Ben Smith Jr. replied, "Can I come with you, Joe Luke?"

Joe Luke shrugged his shoulders. "Yes you can, Ben Smith Jr."

Ben Smith Jr. shook Joe Luke's right hand. "Thank you."

Joe Luke grinned. "You're welcome, Ben Smith Jr."

Ben Smith Jr. helped Joe Luke to go into the saloon.

When they'd entered he said, "Look Joe Luke there's Doc Smith standing up at the bar having a beer."

Joe Luke and Ben Smith Jr. walked up to the counter.

Joe Luke went towards Doc. "Hey, Doc Smith."

Doc Smith turned his head to the left. "Hey, Joe Luke, how are you today?"

Joe Luke leaned on the counter. "I am good."

Doc Smith put his left hand on Joe Luke's right shoulder. "That's good."

Joe Luke turned his neck to the right. "Yep."

Doc Smith looked at Joe Luke. "Hey Joe Luke, what the heck happened to you?"

Joe Luke lifted his hat up on his head. "Frank Cooper Sr. slugged me in the left eye when I hit the ground."

Doc Smith scratched his head. "Ouch. That has to hurt.

"Yep it did, Doc. Oh and this is Ben Smith Jr. , Doc."

Doc Smith spoke, "Nice to meet you Ben Smith Jr." He shook his right hand."

Ben Smith Jr. returned the handshake, "Same with you Doc Smith."

"What have you been doing today, Joe Luke?" said Doc Smith.

"Nothing really, just the law right now." Joe Luke replied.

Doc Smith shrugged his shoulders. "That's cool."

Joe Luke put his left hand out. "Yep it is true."

Ben Smith Jr. put his left hand out. "Are you a doctor here in Dodge City?"

Doc Smith put his right hand out. "Yes I am."

Ben Smith Jr. replied. "Alright."

Doc Smith replied back. "Yep, it is true, Ben Smith Jr."

Chapter 5

Brandi Luke waved her left hand. "Hi, Joe Luke."

Joe Luke waved back with his left hand. "Hey, Brandi Luke.

Brandi Luke replied, "How are you, my husband?"

Joe Luke spoke back. "I am good.

Brandi Luke looked at Joe Luke. "That's good."

Joe Luke smiled at Brandi Luke. "Yep."

Brandi Luke made eye contact with Joe Luke. "Where are you going, my husband?"

Joe Luke glared at Brandi Luke. "I am going to go to go back to the jail."

Brandi Luke smiled. "Can I come with you, my husband?"

Joe Juke shrugged his shoulders. "Sure, my wife."

Joe Luke and Brandi Luke went back to the sheriff's office. It was hard for Joe Luke to go back to the jail with his crutches.

Joe Luke turned his neck to the right. "Okay we are here, my wife."

Brandi Luke spoke, "How are you going to get up those steps with your crutches?"

Joe Luke looked back at Brandi Luke. "Watch me, Brandi." He went up one step and another. All of the sudden Joe Luke fell down all four steps and landed on his right leg. "Ouch! My leg, it hurts."

Brandi Luke looked down at Joe Luke. "Are you alright my husband?"

Joe Luke looked up. "Ya, I will be fine. Brandi can you help me up, please?"

"Sure I can Joe Luke." Brandi Luke bent over and picked her husband off the dirt street.

Joe Luke smiled. "Thank you."

"You're welcome."

Joe Luke opened the sheriff's office door and entered with Brandi.

"Can I have some coffee my husband?" asked Brandi.

Joe Luke smiled. "Sure why not, my wife."

"Where are we going after this my husband?"

Joe Luke shrugged his shoulders. "I guess we can head down to the creek."

Brandi Luke looked at Joe Luke. "Can I come with you?"

Joe Luke shrugged his shoulders again. "Sure. You can ride on my back while hanging on."

Brandi Luke gave Joe Luke a thumbs up. "Okay thank you."

Joe Luke gave Brandi a thumbs up. "You are welcome."

Brandi Luke gave Joe Luke a wink. "Yep."

Joe Luke put his hands up in the air. "Ok."

Brandi Luke smiled. "Ok."

~·~·~

Joe Luke hopped on his horse with his good leg. "Okay Brandi hop on the back of my horse, Lightning."

Joe Luke smiled. "Okay let's ride, Brandi."

Brandi Luke put her left fist in the air. "Sweet."

Joe Luke turned his head to the right. "Hang on to me. Okay here we go, my wife."

Brandi Luke glared at Joe Luke. "To the creek we go."

"Yes indeed my wife."

"Where's the creek at sheriff?"

Joe Luke pointed his finger. "Right over there."

Lightning took them to the creek.

"Okay, Brandi, we are here at the creek alright."

Brandi Luke spoke back. "Okay."

A thinking look crossed Joe Luke's face. "I did not bring my swimming suit."

Brandi Luke had a weird look on her face. "You don't have to, sheriff."

Joe Luke made a weird face. "Why not?"

Brandi Luke put both of her hands up. "Because I am going to push you in the water with my hands now."

"No don't. Oh now what the heck." Joe Luke fell into the creek with his two hands flying way out, and his crutches falling to the ground next to the creek.

Brandi Luke laughed and slapped her hand on her leg. "Ha ha ha ha ha ha ha!"

Joe Luke looked down at his clothes. "I am soaking wet. So are my boots, and my shirt and pants." He slammed his hat into the water.

"How does it feel babe?" asked Brandi.

Joe Luke yelled at Brandi Luke. "I feel terrible Brandi. Thanks a lot for pushing me in the creek."

Brandi Luke saluted. "You are welcome, Joe Luke."

Joe Luke was disappointed. "Now it feels like God thinks I got baptized."

"Ya He does." She said.

Joe Luke got mad. "Get off that horse, Brandi."

Brandi Luke gave Joe Luke a surprised look. "No way, Joe Luke.

No don't, what the heck." Brandi fell off Lightning and into the creek.

Joe Luke laughed, slapping his left hand on his left leg. "Ha ha ha ha ha ha ha ha. You are soaking wet."

"You think." She replied.

"Now God thinks you got baptized as well. Ha ha ha ha ha ha."

~·~·~

Joe Luke and his wife rode back into Dodge.

Deputy Morgan looked up. "Welcome back, Joe Luke and Brandi."

"Thank you, Deputy Morgan," replied Joe Luke.

"Where did you two go this afternoon?"

"We went down to the creek back there."

"I see."

"Yep it's true Deputy Morgan."

Deputy Morgan smiled. "Okay, I see you two are soaking wet."

"How did you know?" Joe Luke asked with a silly grin on his face.

Deputy Morgan put his index finger on the side of his forehead. "I have a good memory, Joe Luke."

"Good to know. Well my wife and I are going to change our clothes."

"Okay have fun you guys."

Joe Luke saluted. "Thank you."

"You are welcome talk to you guys later."

"Ok."

Joe Luke glared at his wife as they rode toward the stable. "Well that was a bad disaster. I look like a dork."

Brandi Luke got off of Joe Luke's horse Lightning. She smiled. "Why is that?"

Joe Luke looked down. "Because I am soaking wet and so is my shirt and pants." He got off of his horse also.

Brandi Luke stared at her husband. "Same here. I love you Joe Luke." She kissed him on the cheek.

Joe Luke smiled. "I love you too," he said while kissing her on the cheek."

Brandi Luke hugged Joe Luke. "Thank you."

Joe Luke hugged his wife back. "You're welcome."

~ ~ ~

Mac Jenkins Sr. held his mouth wide open. "Whoa. What happen to you guys?"

Joe Luke moved his hands around. "Well what happened was my wife pushed me into the creek, my friend."

"I see."

Joe Luke waved. "I guess Brandi and I are going to change our clothes, Mac Jenkins Sr.."

"Okay, injured sheriff with a shot up leg and a black eye."

Joe Luke looked down. "Huh you noticed."

Mac Jenkins Sr. smiled. "Have fun changing your clothes."

Joe Luke grinned. "Thank you."

"You bet."

Joe Luke pointed. "Let's go change our clothes Brandi."

Brandi Luke shrugged her shoulders. "Okay, sounds like a good plan."

"Okay Brandi we will go change our clothes now."

"Let's go change our clothes in your office," she said.

"Are you sure."

"Yes I am sure."

The sheriff and his wife Brandi went to change their clothes in the jail.

Afterward, Brandi said. "Sheriff."

"Yes."

"I am sorry that I pushed you in the creek."

"It's okay. You did not mean it." Joe Luke smiled. "It's ok, and I am also sorry that I pulled you in the creek."

Brandi Luke put her left hand out. "It's okay."

Joe Luke put his left hand out. "Thank you."

Brandi Luke raised her hand up. "You are welcome Joe Luke."

"Yep."

"I am going to go to the saloon now to have a beer, Brandi. Are you going to stay here at the jail or go to the saloon?"

Brandi Luke grinned. "I will stay here."

"Okay if anybody comes to the sheriff's office tell them I am at the Long Branch Saloon, my wife."

"Okay."

"Thank you."

"You are welcome."

~ ~ ~

The sheriff went to the saloon to have a beer with his deputy.

Joe Luke hopped on his crutches while waving his left hand. "Hey, Deputy Morgan."

Deputy Morgan turned his neck to the right. "Hey, sheriff."

"How are you?"

"I am good."

"That's good." Joe Luke smiled.

"Yep it is."

"I am glad.

"My leg hurts awful bad, Deputy Morgan."

The Deputy shrugged. "I am sorry to hear that, Joe Luke."

"It's alright."

Deputy Morgan smiled. "Yep. Where did you go today?"

"My wife and I went down to the creek to look around. Then after that, she pushed me into the creek and I got soaking wet. And now God thinks I got baptized."

"Ha ha ha ha ha ha ha ha. Wow."

"Yep. I pulled her into the creek as well."

Deputy Morgan rested his hands on his belt. "Wow that is something."

"Ya and she totally forgave me for what I did to her.

"Wow, I am glad that she forgave you."

"Yep, I am glad she forgave me for what I did to her at the creek."

"That's good."

Joe Luke nodded. "Yep me too."

"Do you want a beer?"

Joe Luke raised his hat up. "Just one, Deputy Morgan."

Joe Luke spoke to Sam, the bartender. "Thank you."

Sam spoke back to Joe Luke. "You are welcome."

They both drank their beers.

"That hit the spot." said the sheriff.

"That's good." The deputy smiled.

"Yep."

"I will see you later."

"Okay."

Joe Luke saluted Deputy Morgan before going out the saloon doors on his crutches. "Bye."

Deputy Morgan saluted back to Joe Luke. "Bye."

Chapter 6

Billy Bob and Blondy walked up to Mac Jenkins Sr.. "Hi I am Billy Bob and this is my brother Blondy Pattan."

Mac Jenkins Sr. put both of his hands out and shook both of the brothers' hands. "It's nice to meet you both. I am Mac Jenkins Sr., Joe Luke's friend."

"Same with you Mac Jenkins Sr.," Billy Bob and Blondy Pattan chorused.

"Ya."

"Where is Sheriff Joe Luke?" asked Blondy.

"He is chasing this bank robber, Jason, right now."

"When is he going to be back?"

"I don't really know when he is going to be back?"

"Okay, let me know when he is back then," Blondy replied.

"Okay will do."

"Thank you."

"Yep."

~·~·~

Payton Jones walked up to Blondy Pattan with Kayla trailing not too far behind. "What should we do now?"

"I don't know Payton Jones probably wait for Sheriff Joe Luke to get back with the prisoner."

Payton Jones looked up in the sky. "Okay. Well they should be back before the rain comes. I am worried about him because he is, my friend."

Billy Bob shrugged his shoulders. "Same here, Payton Jones."

Payton Jones smiled. "Really?"

Billy Bob smiled back. "Yep. And same with Blondy Pattan too."

Payton gave Billy Bob a wink.

Blondy put his left hand on his face. "What? I felt something land on my face, Billy Bob. I wonder what it is, my brother."

Billy Bob shrugged his shoulders again. "I am not sure. It is dripping on the street in the dirt."

Blondy looked at Billy Bob. "It's true."

Mac Jenkins Sr. stepped out of his shop and was surprised to find Billy Bob and Blondy.

Blondy Pattan pointed his finger. "I just saw lightning in the sky." He looked up. "It's pouring rain."

Mac Jenkins Sr. shouted, "Everybody get off the street now!" He started waving his hands to the side.

Blondy Pattan scratched on top of his head. "I guess we know what was dripping on the street."

Billy Bob scratched his head. "Ya we do, my brother."

Blondy Pattan spoke to Kayla and Payton Jones. "It is pouring rain Kayla and Payton."

Payton's face was filled with excitement. "Oh wow, it is pouring rain real good."

Kayla Jones face was filled with excitement. "Yep it is."

~·~·~

Payton Jones walked up to Billy Bob.

"Where is Sheriff Joe Luke at? He's been gone for a long time."

"Maybe they had to wait out from the storm, Payton Jones" Billy Bob replied.

"That sounds fair with me then. So Sheriff Joe Luke is a friend of yours?"

"He is more than a friend with me and Blondy Pattan."

Payton lifted her eyebrows. "So what would he be to you guys?"

"He would be a brother in the Lord."

"Really I did not know that, Billy Bob and Blondy Pattan."

"Yep it is true, Payton."

"Wow!"

"Yep."

Payton Jones paused a moment. "I did not know that. That is…wow. What are we going to do now, Billy Bob and Blondy Pattan?"

Billy Bob shrugged his shoulders. "I don't know. Wait until the rain quits I guess." He looked at some hard candy in a jar.

Payton Jones spoke, "Okay sounds good then Billy Bob and Blondy Pattan. I hope Joe Luke is doing okay against Jason right now."

Billy Bob raised his two hands in the air. "Me too Payton, me too. And same with Blondy Pattan."

Payton looked up. "Ya, I like Sheriff Joe Luke."

"Ya, how is that Payton?"

"Oh I don't know. He seems to be a nice person."

"Ya same here."

"Really?"

"Yep. It is true. What do you think Payton. Do you think Sheriff Joe Luke is a nice person?"

Payton smiled. "Yep, I do. Because he is a good friend."

"Ya same here. Blondy Pattan and I are really good friends with Sheriff Joe Luke, so that's good."

"Yep it is. So how come sheriff Joe Luke has a wife Billy Bob?"

"I have no idea Payton maybe he wants to, I guess." Billy Bob shrugged his shoulders.

"I see."

"Yep it is true Kayla and Payton."

"I don't have to bug him anymore then. That is great." Payton pointed her finger at Joe Luke's friend Billy Bob.

"What do you mean Payton?"

Payton Jones glared. "What do I mean? Well you see I don't really care if he has a wife or not."

Billy Bob replied. "I see."

Payton Jones replied. "Yep all I care about is him being, my friend so ya that's why Billy Bob."

Mac Jenkins Sr. pointed out the window. "Look, sheriff Joe Luke is back. I am glad he caught the robber."

Everyone filed out of the hardware store.

Ben Smith Jr. smiled. "Me to, Mac Jenkins Sr.."

Duke Owens raised his left fist in the air. "Right on, Sheriff Joe Luke. You caught him, my friend."

Joe Luke rode up next to Duke Owens with a smile. "Thank you Duke Owens."

Duke Owens answered. "You are so welcome, my friend what are you going to do now Joe Luke."

"Probably nothing.

"What are you going to do with him?"

"I am taking him to jail now."

"Okay see you later, sheriff."

Joe Luke raised a finger. "Quick question."

"What is it?"

"How come it's raining here in Dodge City?"

"I don't know maybe it wants to I guess. Owens shrugged his shoulders at Joe Luke.

"I see."

"Yep."

"I hate rain right now, Duke Owens."

"Really?"

"Yep, it's true, my friend what are you going to do now Duke Owens?"

"I am heading back to the Dodge House."

"Okay, see you later then."

"Okay."

Joe Luke saluted. "Bye, Duke Owens."

"Bye, Joe Luke."

"See you later."

"Okay." Duke Owens saluted back at his awesome friend, Joe Luke.

"See you later." Joe Luke gave Duke Owens an awesome wave.

~ · ~ · ~

"Sheriff Joe Luke."

"Ya Billy Bob."

"What are you going to do with Jason?"

"I am going to take him to jail." Joe Luke pointed jail ward.

"Okay sounds like that should be fun, my friend."

"Ya it should be fun, my friend."

Billy Bob smiled. "We will grab something to eat."

"Okay sounds good then," said Joe Luke.

Joe Luke shoved Jason into the muddy road with his left hand. "Come on Jason Smith let's go."

Joe Luke motioned his finger. "Deputy."

Deputy Morgan came over to Joe Luke. "Ya."

Joe Luke begged to Deputy Morgan, "Please take Jason Smith to jail for me."

Deputy Morgan puffed his chest out. "Sure thing sheriff."

"Thank you."

"Yep."

"I will see you later, Deputy Morgan."

Deputy Morgan replied. "Okay Sheriff see you back at the sheriff's office."

Joe Luke winked. "Okay, Deputy Morgan."

Billy Bob ran over to Joe Luke. "Joe Luke."

Sheriff Joe Luke turned to Billy Bob. "Ya."

Billy Bob asked. "What are you going to do now?"

"I am going to the saloon I guess."

"Okay, I will come with you then."

Joe Luke replied. "Okay, Billy Bob."

~'~'~

Back at the Long Branch Saloon.

Bob Peck pointed at Bill Smith Sr. "Hey, you with the hat."

Bill Smith Sr. pointed his finger back at him. "Who me?"

Bob Peck spoke to Bill Smith Sr. with a mean look on his face. "Ya you."

Bill Smith Sr. pointed his finger at Bob Peck. "What do you want?"

"You killed my brother didn't you?"

"What would I do that for, Bob Peck?"

"You tell me, Bill Smith Sr."

Bill Smith Sr. put his right hand on his six gun and he was about to draw his gun out of his holster. "Now draw that gun of yours right now."

Bob Peck clenched his right fist at Bill Smith Sr. "The sheriff will put you in jail."

"No he won't, Bob."

"Yep he will."

Joe Luke hopped into the saloon on his crutches. "No I won't Bob. Bill did not kill your brother."

Bob Peck spoke, "Well if it isn't the injured, black eye sheriff, Joe Luke. The hero that brought the robber to justice. Who killed my brother, Joe Luke?"

Joe Luke smiled. "You killed your own brother, Bob."

Bob Peck put both of his hands up in the air. "What? I did not. Payton Jones killed my brother in cold blood."

"What is your brother's name, Bob Peck."

"My brother's name is Tom Peck."

"Really!"

"Yep it is sheriff."

"Wow I did not know that, Bob Peck."

"Yep it is true, Sheriff."

Joe Luke rubbed his chin. "I see. But I still don't have proof that Payton killed your brother, Bob."

"You have to have proof sheriff."

Joe Luke put both of his hands out. "Well I don't Bob, so just leave this to me. Alright, Bob Peck."

Bob Peck raised his left hand up at Joe Luke. "Okay, whatever, Joe Luke. Do what you want, sheriff Joe Luke."

Joe Luke gave Bob Peck a mean look. "Fine. I will you jerk."

"Did you just called me a jerk?"

"I did."

"Draw that gun of yours sheriff."

Joe Luke reached for his six gun and he was about to draw it. "I am not going to draw against you, Bob the tin horn jerk.

Bob Peck reached for his six gun and he was about to draw. "That's it. Let's see how good you are sheriff.

Joe Luke drew his six gun. "No don't."

Bang.

Bob Peck fell to his knees. "You never gave me a chance, sheriff."

Joe Luke looked down. "I never did, and I wasn't going to either."

Bob Peck looked up. "I hate you."

Joe Luke glared. "I don't really care Bob."

Billy Bob looked down. "Is he dead?"

Joe Luke smiled. "Ya he deserved it, my friend."

"Ya he did. What now sheriff?"

"I guess I will go to my sheriff's office now. Okay let me know if you see any trouble Billy Bob and Blondy Pattan."

"Will do."

Joe Luke saluted. "Thank you guys."

Billy Bob saluted. "You are welcome."

Chapter 7

Joe Luke hopped out of the saloon on the dirt street with his crutches.

Payton Jones waved her hands at Joe Luke. "Sheriff. Sheriff."

Joe Luke looked over and saw Payton. "Yes, Payton."

"There is a little boy right here in the ally next to the Long Branch Saloon."

"What happened?"

"He's been hit in the head with a gun, come quick you better kneel down."

Joe Luke hopped over to the alley next to the Long Branch Saloon to kneel down and he saw blood on the back of the boys head. "He's dead."

Payton Jones pulled her pistol out of the holster and lift her right hand up in the air.

Joe Luke raised his head up. "Huh?"

Payton Jones hit Joe Luke in the head. He crumpled to the ground.

Payton Jones saluted. "You won't be killing no bad guys now, Joe Luke. See you later." She slipped his gun out of his holster. "You won't be needing your gun anymore. Bye sheriff. I won't be seen you around anymore."

Payton Jones walked in her little house.

Payton waved. "Hey Kayla."

Kayla saluted. "Hey Payton. What's happening?"

Payton Jones lifted both of her hands up in the air. "I hit sheriff on the back of his head with my gun."

"What? Why did you do that for?"

Payton Jones shrugged her shoulders back. "Because I felt like it, Kayla. I am a bad girl and I am evil too. Ha ha ha ha ha."

Kayla put her hands on her hips. "That's not funny, Payton."

Payton Jones put her hands on her hips. "It is to me, Kayla Jones."

Kayla Jones replied, "Why is that, Payton Jones."

"I don't know, Kayla."

"You know Joe Luke is going to put you in jail, Payton."

"I don't think so, Kayla."

"Why?"

Payton Jones raised her left hand in the air. "Because I am not going to jail ever. And that is why I am not going."

"But you hit Joe Luke in the head with your six gun, Payton."

"So what is your point, Kayla?"

"I don't know, Payton."

"That's right you don't have a point, Kayla."

Kayla Jones looked at her sister. "Joe Luke killed our cousin, Hank Jones, not too long ago, Payton."

Payton Jones made a mean look at Kayla. "Ya, and Joe Luke is going to pay for killing my cousin, Hank Jones."

~·~·~

Back at the Long Branch Saloon two drunken cowboys walked out the saloon doors and walked next to the alley and saw a body lying on the ground.

Mac Jenkins Sr. in a strangely slurred voice said, "Hey look. It's

Joe Luke. He's been hit in the head with something."

John Cooper and Mac Jenkins Sr. said in unison. "Yep with a gun. Wow, wow."

"Let's take him up to Docs office Mac Jenkins Sr.," Mr. Coper slurred.

"Sure thing John Cooper," Mac Jenkins Sr. said with a salute.

Mac Jenkins Sr. and John Cooper took Joe Luke to Docs office.

~·~·~

Mac Jenkins Sr. knocked on the door. "Doc, are you there."

"Ya, I am here. What is it Mac Jenkins Sr.?" Dock opened the door. "Come on in you guys."

Mac Jenkins Sr., and Mr. Cooper walked in carrying Joe Luke. They set him on the table.

"Joe Luke has been hit in the head with a gun," said Mac Jenkins Sr.. "What are you going to do Doc Smith?"

"I am going to check his heartrate and a few other body parts."

Mac Jenkins Sr. smiled. "Okay keep us posted on Joe Luke, Doc Smith."

Doc Smith smiled back. "Sure thing Mac Jenkins Sr.."

John Cooper shook Doc Smiths hand. "I am John Cooper."

Doc Smith shook his hand back. "Nice to meet you John Cooper, my name is Doc Smith."

"Nice to meet you as well, Doc Smith."

"Thank you, John Cooper."

"You are welcome, Doc Smith."

~·~·~

Mac Jenkins Sr. walked inside the Long Branch Saloon.

Samantha Reed walked up to him. "Mac Jenkins Sr.."

Mac Jenkins Sr. stopped walking. "Yes, Samantha Reed."

"Where's Joe Luke."

"He's in Doc Smiths office getting his heartrate done."

"What is he doing over there?"

"Somebody hit him in the head with a six gun."

"Ouch."

"Ya. He is alright but he has a concussion on his head."

"Okay thank you Mac Jenkins Sr.."

"You bet Samantha."

"Let me know how he is doing then."

"Okay sounds good then Samantha Reed."

Mac Jenkins Sr. walked outside the saloon doors and saw Doc Smith out of the corner of his eye.

Doc Smith walked up to him. "Mac Jenkins Sr.."

Mac Jenkins Sr. turned around. "Yes, Doc Smith."

"What are you going to do now?"

"I am going back to my hardware store. Why?"

"Just wondering."

"Okay."

"Have fun at your shop, Mac Jenkins Sr.." Doc Smith said with a wave.

Mac Jenkins Sr. saluted. "Thank you."

Doc Smith saluted. "You are welcome."

~ ~ ~

Deputy Morgan walked through the Long Branch Saloon doors and saw Samantha Reed sitting at the table.

Deputy Morgan shrugged. "I think I know who hit Joe Luke in the head.

Samantha Reed gave Deputy Morgan a surprised look on her face. "Who Deputy Morgan!"

"Payton Jones hit Joe Luke in the head."

"How is the little boy Deputy Morgan?"

"The little boy is dead. There is blood on the back of his head."

"Ouch."

"See you later. I am going to see how Joe Luke is, Samantha Reed."

Samantha smiled and said with a wave. "Okay then."

The deputy saluted. "Bye, Samantha Reed."

Samantha Reed saluted back. "Bye, Deputy Morgan."

~ ' ~ ~

At the Docs office Joe Luke got out of bed.

Deputy Morgan knocked. "Doc?"

Doc Smith spoke while opening the door again, "Yes Deputy Morgan? Come in."

"How is Joe Luke doing, Doc?"

"Good. He is out of bed."

Deputy Morgan wiped his right hand on his head. "That's good."

"Yep." Replied Doc Smith.

"Can I talk to him."

"Sure."

"Thank you."

"You are welcome Deputy Morgan."

Deputy Morgan entered the back room where Joe Luke was.

Joe Luke saluted. "Hey, Deputy Morgan."

Deputy Morgan saluted back. "Hey, Joe Luke. I know who it you in the head and killed the little boy."

"Who Deputy Morgan?"

"Payton Jones killed the little boy and hit you in the head."

Joe Luke patted Deputy Morgan on the shoulder. "Thanks for letting me know, Deputy Morgan."

Deputy Morgan saluted back. "You are welcome, Joe Luke."

Chapter 8

Deputy Morgan rushed though the jail door and smiled. "Joe Luke are you there?" He shut the door behind him.

Joe Luke smiled back. "Ya, I am here Deputy Morgan. What is it?"

"Payton Jones is in town, Joe Luke."

"Okay thank you for letting me know Deputy Morgan." He scratched his head.

"You bet, Joe Luke. Just doing my duty."

"Okay."

"What are you going to do Joe Luke?"

"I am going to have my revenge on Payton Jones."

"Sounds like a plan, Joe Luke."

"Help me Deputy Morgan." He yelled.

"Okay."

"Where's my six gun, Deputy Morgan?" Joe Luke looked all over in the jail.

Deputy Morgan shrugged his shoulders. "I don't know. Here, use my six gun, Joe Luke."

"Thank you Deputy Morgan," he said with a salute.

The deputy saluted back. "You are welcome Joe Luke."

~'~'~

Joe Luke walked out of the jail and hopped towards Payton Jones.

Joe Luke yelled out. "Payton."

Payton yelled back with a mean look. "What, Joe Luke?"

The sheriff shrugged both arms. "Why did you hit me in the head with your six gun?"

"I don't know Joe Luke. You are hard to get rid of."

Joe Luke yelled back. "You have to have a reason to hit me in the head."

Payton Jones pointed. "You killed my cousin Hank Jones, Joe Luke."

Joe Luke rubbed his chin. "I see."

Payton Jones gave Joe Luke a thinking look. "Yep, it's true Joe Luke. What happens if I pulled my six gun out of my holster Joe Luke."

"Then I will shoot your six gun out of your right hand if I have to."

"You try me Joe Luke. Let's see how brave you are." Replied Payton Jones.

"No don't Payton Jones."

Bang.

"What heck Joe Luke. You shot my gun out of my right hand and injured it!"

"I am glad." Joe Luke put both hands behind his back. "Now I am placing you under arrest for the murder of the little boy that you killed today. Deputy Morgan, take her into custody."

"I hope you get sprayed by a skunk Joe Luke."

"Ha ha ha ha ha ha ha. How cute, Payton."

"Thank you Joe Luke."

"Ya whatever."

A skunk came into Dodge City to find Joe Luke.

Billy Bob yelled with excitement. "It's a skunk! Run! "

Payton Jones looked up. "Maybe it's looking for you, Joe Luke."

"Ha ha ha ha ha ha ha ha ha. Very funny, Payton," the sheriff replied with an ordinary voice.

Joe Luke smiled. "I am going to distract the skunk so that way it can leave Dodge City Mac Jenkins Sr.."

Mac Jenkins Sr. smiled back. "Sounds like a plan Joe Luke. However, I am worried about you getting sprayed, Joe Luke."

Joe Luke said, "Don't worry. I will get use to the smell Mac Jenkins Sr.."

"If you get sprayed by a skunk, are you going to get your dog, Joe?"

"No. That's why I got you, Mac Jenkins Sr.."

"Okay Joe Luke, sounds like a plan."

"Okay thank you, Mac Jenkins Sr.."

"You are welcome, Joe Luke. You are a good friend."

"Same with you Mac Jenkins Sr. I can't wait to do our skunk hunting." Joe Luke threw his hat in the air, "Yee-Haw!"

Mac Jenkins Sr. raised his fist in the air. "That's right, Joe Luke! Yee-Haw is correct."

Joe Luke put both hands out. "Yep it is, Mac Jenkins Sr.."

The skunk walked into the street.

Joe Luke spoke, "It's a skunk. Everybody hide in the buildings, now."

Joe Luke and Mac Jenkins Sr. and everybody else ran inside the buildings where it was safe.

Joe Luke shrugged his shoulders. "What now, Mac Jenkins Sr.? I guess we will wait until the skunk goes by."

Mac Jenkins Sr. shrugged his shoulders back. "What happens if the skunk does go by?"

"Then I guess we will sneak out the back door, Mac Jenkins Sr.."

Mac Jenkins Sr. gulped because he was nervous to go outside to find the skunk. "Okay sounds good to me then, Joe Luke."

Joe Luke smiled at Mac Jenkins Sr.. "Alright let's do this, Mac Jenkins Sr.."

Mac Jenkins Sr. looked over at Joe Luke. "Okay do you see anything, sheriff."

Joe Luke looked up at Mac Jenkins Sr.. "Nope. That's why I got my six gun out, Mac Jenkins Sr.."

"I see."

"Yep."

Joe Luke got up and motioned Mac Jenkins Sr. to follow him. He went out the back door. "Okay. Let's go. Okay I will peek around the corner, Mac Jenkins Sr.."

Mac Jenkins Sr. grinned. "Okay."

Joe Luke pointed. "Let's go peek around this corner."

Mac Jenkins Sr. shrugged his shoulders. "What happened to the skunk?"

"I don't know, Mac Jenkins Sr.."

"You don't think the skunk left Dodge City, do you think, Joe Luke?"

"I am not sure, Mac Jenkins Sr.."

"Okay."

Joe Luke pointed. "I will go right and you go left and we will meet back here at your hardware store."

"Okay, Joe Luke, sounds like a plan."

"Okay good luck, Mac Jenkins Sr.."

"Same with you, sheriff."

Joe Luke saluted. "Thank you."

Mac Jenkins Sr. saluted back. "You are welcome, Joe Luke."

~·~·~

Deputy Morgan ran towards the Sheriff. "Joe Luke."

Joe Luke turned his neck around to the left toward Deputy Morgan. "Yes Deputy."

Deputy Morgan replied. "Payton is in jail now."

"Okay thank you."

"What are you doing?"

"I am going to kill this skunk."

Deputy Morgan saluted. "Well, have fun Sheriff."

Joe Luke saluted back. "Thank you, Deputy."

Deputy Morgan nodded his head. "You are welcome, Sheriff."

Joe Luke hopped around with his crutches, "Here skunky, skunky. Where are you big kitty cat."

Mac Jenkins Sr. yelled, "Joe Luke, help me I found the skunk!

Joe Luke yelled back. "I'm coming, Mac Jenkins Sr.!" Joe Luke smiled. "Where at Mac Jenkins Sr.?"

Joe Luke hopped around to the left with his crutches when he saw Mac Jenkins Sr. at the horse stable.

Mac Jenkins Sr. pointed. "Right here beside the horse stable, in front of me."

Joe Luke put his right hand out. "Just a second, Mac Jenkins Sr.. Here I am, Mac Jenkins Sr.."

Mac Jenkins Sr. lifted his right hand up in the air. "Do not move, Joe Luke."

Joe Luke froze a moment in front of the horse stable. He made a weird face. "Why?"

Mac Jenkins Sr. pointed down. "The skunk is right next to you."

Joe Luke put his crutches in front of the horse stable and kneeled down. He placed his left hand in the dirt next to the skunk's front foot. He fired three shots in front of the skunk, giving it a warning.

The skunk was mad and stomped its right front foot at Joe Luke. The skunk raised its tail up and turned its hind end around towards Joe Luke's face.

Mac Jenkins Sr. backed up and Joe Luke got nailed twice in the face.

Mac Jenkins Sr. rubbed his chin. "I got an idea!"

Joe Luke rolled around in the dirt to try to get the skunk smell off of his face. "Okay what are you going to do, Mac Jenkins Sr.?"

Mac Jenkins Sr. put his left hand out. "I am going to get your dog, Joe the rat/skunk terrier."

Joe Luke raised his thumb up and sputtered. "Okay, sounds good to me then."

Mac Jenkins Sr. ran. "Be right back."

Joe Luke nodded his head. "Okay."

The skunk came over to Joe Luke again and sprayed him eight more times in the face.

Mac Jenkins Sr. opened the sheriff's jail door. "Joe. Come here, I have a surprise for you dog." Joe came up to Mac Jenkins Sr.. "Let's go where Joe Luke is." Mac Jenkins Sr. and Joe ran over to the horse stable. "This is your dog, Joe."

"Yep."

"Nice. Look at your dog it is chasing the skunk out of Dodge. Sweet! Oh, he got sprayed fifteen times.

"I can't see. I got skunk oil in my eyes. Mac Jenkins Sr.."

"Okay, Joe Luke, well your dog is coming back now.

"That's good Mac Jenkins Sr.. I want him to come back.

Mac Jenkins Sr. wiped his head. "Yep it is, Joe Luke."

~·~·~

Billy Bob looked around town. "Sheriff?"

Joe Luke turned around. "Yes, Billy Bob?"

Billy Bob put both hands on his belt buckle. "Is the skunk gone?" Joe Luke yelled. "I hope the skunk never comes back."

Billy Bob covered the top of his face. "Yep I hope not, Joe Luke. Because you smell bad".

Joe Luke was disappointed. "I am sorry Billy Bob."

"It's okay."

"Me to Billy Bob."

"Yep…What now?"

"I am going to my office right now to see my deputy, okay? See you later, Billy Bob."

"Bye, Sheriff." Billy Bob held out his right hand. "You are a good, friend Sheriff."

Joe Luke nodded. "You to, Billy Bob."

"Thank you, Sheriff."

"You are welcome, Billy Bob.

"Yep."

Joe Luke was blind when he hit the store posts one after another while heading back to the office to see his Deputy.

~·~·~

Joe Luke entered the jail.

Deputy Morgan waved. "Hello, sheriff."

Joe Luke waved back. "Hi, Deputy."

Deputy Morgan covered his nose. "What happened to you?

"I got spayed ten times total in the face by a skunk; and I am blind too."

"I am sorry to hear that, Joe Luke."

Joe Luke spoke back, "It's okay, Deputy Morgan."

"How did you do on your skunk job?"

"Good. My dog chased him out of Dodge and he got sprayed by a skunk fifteen Times total."

Mac Jenkins Sr. looked up from some paperwork, "Wow! Where is your dog now?"

"He is outside right now."

"That's good. He needs to stay outside if he smells bad."

"Sounds good then, Deputy Morgan."

"How's Payton doing right here in jail?"

"Not very good sheriff. She hates been here in jail."

"I don't care for that little tin horn because she killed the little boy next to the Long Branch Saloon."

"I can't believe it though."

Joe Luke grimaced. "Ya I agree with you, Deputy Morgan."

Deputy Morgan grimaced back. "Thank you, Sheriff."

"You are welcome Deputy."

Joe Luke crawled towards his bed where the back door was, trying his best to find it. "Yep. Well, I am going to take a nap now."

Deputy Morgan nodded. "Okay."

"Wake me up if there is any noise."

Deputy Morgan rubbed his face with his left hand. "Okay, sounds good to me then, Sheriff. I will let you know then."

Joe Luke rubbed his right hand on his face and wiped some of the skunk smell off his face. "Okay."

"I won't bug you now."

"Okay go to the saloon and have a beer, Deputy. And let me know what happens."

Deputy Morgan headed out the sheriff office's door. "Okay."

Chapter 9

In the street near the sheriff's office, Ben Smith Jr. spoke to everybody. "The same train is back here in Dodge."

Bill Smith Sr. jumped up in the air. "Sweet."

Ben Smith Jr. motioned. "Bring those mules over here to the Santa Fe train. Let's unload the money and the supplies to Mac Jenkins Sr. hardware store."

Bill Smith Sr. waved. "Sure thing, Ben Smith Jr."

~ ~ ~

Deputy Morgan walked in the saloon.

Samantha Reed waved. "Hey, Deputy Morgan."

Deputy Morgan waved back. "Hey, Samantha. How are you today?"

"I am good, Deputy."

"That's good."

"Yep. How are you, Deputy Morgan."

"I am good, Samantha."

"That's good."

"Yep it is, Samantha." Deputy Morgan turned to Sam Jr. who is behind the bar. "I guess I will have a beer, Sam Jr."

Sam Jr. winked. "Okay, Deputy. I will bring it right out."

Deputy Morgan saluted. "Thank you."

Sam Jr. set the beer on the table in front of Deputy Morgan. "Here is your beer, Deputy."

Deputy Morgan waved. "Thank you, Sam Jr."

Sam Jr. waved back. "You are welcome, Deputy." He walked back to the counter.

Deputy Morgan pointed down. "This is good beer, Samantha."

Samantha Reed got out of her seat. "Thank you, Deputy."

"You are welcome Samantha. Wow, that hit the spot right there." He patted his belly.

"Do you want another beer?" asked Samantha.

"Maybe just one more will be good for me then, Samantha."

Samantha Reed spoke, "Sam."

Sam Jr. turned his neck towards Samantha Reed. "Ya."

Samantha raised her index finger in the air. "Bring the, deputy one more beer."

Sam Jr. nodded. "Okay."

Deputy Morgan looked at Sam Jr. "Thank you, Sam."

Sam Jr. looked at Deputy Morgan. "You are welcome, Deputy."

Sam Jr. set the beer on the table in front of him. "There you go Deputy Morgan. Here is your other beer."

Deputy Morgan looked up at Sam Jr., "Thank you, Sam Jr."

Sam Jr. looked down at Deputy Morgan. "You are welcome."

~·~·~

Sam Jr. opened the back door to get another barrel of beer.

Bang. Bang.

Deputy Morgan looked behind him. "What the heck."

Samantha Reed looked in front of the saloon doors. "What was that?"

Deputy Morgan and Samantha Reed looked at each other. "I don't know Mrs. Reed. I think it came from outside."

"Let's go check it out."

"Okay sounds good then."

Everybody rushed out the saloon doors with Deputy Morgan.

Deputy Morgan looked down. "What the?"

Mack Jenkins Jr. looked at Him. "What is it Deputy."

"A man is lying on the ground you guys go get Doc and the sheriff."

"Yes sir."

"Thank you."

"Yep."

~ ~ ~

Mack Jenkins Jr. ran over to the sheriff's office to get Joe Luke. "Sheriff."

Joe Luke fell off of his bed onto the ground. "Ya."

"Somebody has been shot in front of the Long Branch Saloon."

Joe Luke got up off the dirty ground, brushing off his freshly clean clothes. "Okay I will go check it out now. Lucky for you I just took a bath to wash of the skunk smell with tomato juice."

"Okay, Sheriff. I will come with you."

"Okay sounds good then, Mack Jenkins Jr."

Mack Jenkins Jr. helped Joe Luke walk towards the Long Branch Saloon.

Joe Luke hopped over to everybody and kneeled down. "Okay what do we have here? This guy is Billy Jenkins."

Mack Jenkins Jr. was surprised. "Really now?"

Joe Luke raised his head up. "Yep."

Mack Jenkins Jr. gasped. "I did not know that."

Joe Luke raised both hands in the air. "It's true, Mack Jenkins Jr."

Mack Jenkins Jr. was shocked. "Wow!"

Deputy Morgan put his two hands on his knees. "Looks like he has been shot in the back five times, Joe Luke.

Joe Luke put his right knee on the ground while rolling the body over. "What!" He looked up. "Did anybody see what happened?"

Mack Jenkins Jr. looked down. "No sir we were all in the saloon when this happened."

Joe Luke put his left hand on his left leg. "I see. Well I will try my best to see who shot this man in the back."

Mack Jenkins Jr. rubbed his chin. "You better, sheriff."

Joe Luke got up. "I will, don't worry you guys."

Mack Jenkins Jr. raised his two hands up in the air. "Okay."

Deputy Morgan made eye contact. "Sheriff."

Joe Luke turned his neck to the left. "Ya, Deputy?"

"How are you going to find this killer?

"I am not sure, Deputy."

"Oh okay. I was just wondering so.

"Okay that's fine, Deputy."

"I think I will go back to the saloon to finish my beer, sheriff."

"Okay and after that I am going to need your help finding this killer, Deputy."

"Sure thing, Sheriff."

"Okay Deputy. See you then."

"Okay, sheriff."

Joe Luke saluted. "Alright see you at the sheriff's office then."

Deputy Morgan saluted. "Okay."

⁓˙⁓˙⁓

Samantha Reed looked up. "He needs your help to find this killer."

Deputy Morgan looked down. "Yep he does, Samantha."

"Okay. Well good luck to you and the sheriff," said Samantha.

"Thank you, Samantha." Said Deputy Morgan.

"You are welcome, Deputy Morgan."

"Well, thank you for the beer, Samantha."

"You are welcome, Deputy Morgan."

Deputy Morgan winked. "I better get back to the sheriff's office where the sheriff is. Talk to you later Samantha."

Samantha Reed winked back. "Okay bye."

~·~·~

Deputy Morgan walked over to the sheriff's office and opened the door. He peeked inside. "I am here, Joe Luke."

Joe Luke gave Deputy Morgan a happy look. "Good I am glad you are here, Deputy."

"I see."

"Are you ready to find this killer?"

"I guess. But you are partially blind, sir."

"So you can help me out side with the posse."

"But you smell bad, Joe Luke."

Joe Luke put both hands on his hips. "I don't care, Deputy Morgan. We have a posse outside waiting for us."

"I saw that sheriff so that's good."

"Yep it is good. Jesus Christ believes in us and he is wishing us luck, deputy."

"That's good."

Joe Luke spoke out. "Yep it is. And also praise the Lord that we will try our best to get this killer."

Deputy Morgan raised his finger in the air. "Yes indeed, Sheriff.

Chapter 10

Joe Luke, Deputy Morgan, Billy Jenkins Jr., and Joe Cooper sat in the shreriff's office.

Joe Luke moved his hands around. "Okay I guess we can go find this killer, Deputy Morgan."

"Okay let's go then."

Joe Luke stepped outside the jail door. "Hey guys let's walk around town and see if we can try to find this killer, shall we."

Bill Smith Sr. shrugged his shoulders. "Sure. Why not, Sheriff."

Deputy Morgan motioned. "Okay let's go then."

Joe Luke spread both of his hands out. "Okay everyone spread out."

Joe Cooper saluted. "Yes sir, we sure can, Sheriff."

Joe Luke spoke back. "Okay good luck to you guys."

Joe Cooper replied. "You too, Joe Luke."

"Thank you, Joe Cooper."

Joe Cooper smiled. "Yep, Sure thing."

"Okay let us know if you guys have seen anything yet," called Joe Luke.

Mac Jenkins Sr. replied back. "Okay will do, Sheriff."

~·~·~

Joe Luke and Deputy Morgan walked around town.

Joe Luke motioned. "Okay, come on, Deputy."

Joe Luke turned his neck. "Okay do you see anything?"

Deputy Morgan shook his head. "Nope, not yet, sir."

Joe Luke whispered. "Okay keep your eyes peeled, Deputy.

Deputy Morgan whispered back. "I will, Sheriff."

Joe Luke and Deputy Morgan spread out to find the killer.

"Okay Deputy Morgan," Joe Luke called.

"Bark, Bark."

Joe Luke and Deputy Morgan turned around at the hardware store. "What the?"

Joe Luke heard Joe, the skunk terrier, bark twice. "That's Joe barking at something."

Joe Luke and Deputy Morgan ran over to Joe the skunk terrier at the jail.

Deputy Morgan said, "Ya he is. But at what though, Joe Luke? Let's go check it out then."

Joe Luke shrugged his shoulders back. "Okay sounds good to me then."

Deputy Morgan saluted. "Okay, Joe Luke."

"Well I don't see anything yet."

"Neither do I sheriff," replied Deputy Morgan.

Joe Luke looked down at his dog. "Ya don't bark unless you see something, dog. Let's go back to the hardware store."

~·~·~

Ben Smith Jr. walked up to Joe Luke and Deputy Morgan at the hardware store.

Ben Smith Jr. spoke, "Joe Luke."

Joe Luke turned his neck. "Ya, Ben Smith Jr."

Ben Smith Jr. pointed behind him. "We got one man down."

Joe Luke scratched his head. "Where at, Ben Smith Jr.?"

"In the horse stable, Joe Luke."

"Okay I am heading there now."

Joe Luke, Ben Smith Jr. and Deputy Morgan walked towards the horse stable.

"Where is he, Ben?" asked Joe Luke.

"Right here, Joe Luke. In front of the door."

Joe knelt down and turned the body over. "It's Henry Sr." He checked for a pulse to see if he was still alive. "Take him up to Docs office right now."

Ben Smith Jr. saluted. "Yes, sir."

Joe Luke saluted back. "Thank you, Ben."

"Yep I will see you and Deputy Morgan in a second, Sheriff."

Ben Smith Jr. took Henry Sr. to Docs office.

Joe Luke turned his neck to Deputy Morgan and smiled. "Okay that should keep him busy for a while, Deputy Morgan."

Deputy Morgan rubbed his chin. "Ya that should keep him busy for a while. Sheriff, let's get back to finding this killer."

Joe Luke rubbed his face. "Sure thing, Deputy Morgan. We have to have the killer show his face sometime today."

"Sheriff, you are right."

"Thank you."

~ ~ ~

Ben Smith Jr. walked up to Joe Luke and Deputy Morgan at the horse stable.

Ben Smith Jr. said, "Sheriff."

Joe Luke put both of his hands on his gun belt. "Yes, Ben?"

"Doc told me that Henry Sr. died."

Joe Luke lifted his hat up on his head. "That's a shame. He was a really good man Ben Smith Jr. Let's go catch ourselves a killer."

Ben Smith Jr. took off to look for the killer.

"Yee-Haw there goes Ben Smith Jr." said Deputy Morgan.

"Yep when I die, I want him to be a US Marshal," replied Joe Luke.

"Sure thing Joe Luke," replied Deputy Morgan.

"Thank you, Deputy Morgan."

"You are welcome, Sheriff Joe Luke."

"Let's go protect Dodge City. Yee-Haw, Deputy Morgan."

Deputy Morgan tilted his head to the right. "Really?"

"Yep, that's what I want to say, Deputy Morgan."

"I see sheriff I want to say, 'Yee-Haw' too."

"Are you sure you want to say that?"

Deputy Morgan put both of his hands on his gun belt. "That's what I want to say."

Joe Luke made eye contact. "I see Deputy Morgan."

Deputy Morgan lifted his hat up on his head. "Yep it's true, Joe Luke. How are we going to catch this killer?"

Joe Luke shrugged. "I am not sure, Deputy Morgan."

"I see."

"Yep let's keep our eyes peeled, Deputy Morgan."

"Sure thing, Joe Luke."

"Okay."

"I guess we don't know what the killer looks like."

"That's right, Deputy Morgan."

"Wow, I can't believe I was right on that one, Joe Luke."

"Yep." Joe Luke smiled.

"What is taking the killer so long to show his face?"

"I don't know, Deputy Morgan."

"Maybe he doesn't want to get caught. I wonder who the next target is ,Sheriff?"

"I am not sure, Deputy Morgan."

"Wow! There is nothing here Joe Luke!"

"Same here, Deputy Morgan."

Deputy Morgan rubbed his face. "I can't believe that nobody is here."

Joe Luke replied. "I know, Deputy Morgan."

Ben Smith Jr. walked up to Joe Luke. "Sheriff."

Joe Luke looked over at Ben Smith Jr. "Yes, Ben."

"The men and I don't see anything yet."

"Okay keep your eyes peeled, Ben."

Ben Smith Jr. saluted. "Yes sir, we will."

~·~·~

Joe Luke looked back at his Deputy. He whispered. "Anything yet, Deputy Morgan."

Deputy Morgan whispered back. "Not yet, sheriff."

"Okay keep your eyes peeled, Deputy Morgan."

"Will do sheriff. We need to find out this guy's name in order to bring him to justice. "To bad we don't have any witnesses."

"That's right Deputy Morgan we don't have any wittnesses."

"What now, Sheriff?"

"I am not sure. Maybe we will have to wait till he strikes again."

Deputy Morgan nodded. "Sounds good to me sheriff."

"Okay Deputy Morgan."

"Sheriff. This is a waste of time."

"Why is that, Deputy Morgan?"

Deputy Morgan shrugged his shoulders. "I don't know, sheriff. You don't want to head back to the sheriff's office, but I can't let you die."

Joe Luke shrugged his shoulders back. "I am going to die sooner or later, Deputy Morgan."

"You are not going to die for a very long time, my friend."

"I see how come you don't want me to die here in Dodge City."

"Because you are a good sheriff."

"So what is today, Deputy Morgan?"

"Today is December twenty fifth, eighteen seventy-six."

"I am forty years old, Deputy Morgan."

"Wow sheriff! Forty years old. That's still young."

"Ya it is, Deputy Morgan."

Deputy Morgan made a weird face. "Does the killer know you are forty years old?"

Joe Luke made a weird face back. "Probably not, Deputy Morgan."

Joe Luke stretched. "All we have to think about is the killer, Deputy."

Deputy Morgan raised his hands up in the air. "Okay, Sheriff. Whatever you say."

~ ~ ~

Ben Smith Jr. walked up and cut in on the conversation with Joe Luke and Deputy Morgan. "Sheriff we have another man down."

Joe Luke turned his neck. "Where is he at, Ben?"

"My men are taking care of him right now."

"Where was he at, Ben?"

"He was shot in the alley right next to the hardware store, Sheriff?"

"Thank you for letting me know, Ben."

"You are welcome, Sheriff."

Joe Luke nodded. "Did anyone see the shooter, Ben?"

Ben shook his head. "No, I haven't talked to all the witnesses yet. But I will get right on that. I'll be at the jail if you find anything out, sheriff."

"Okay Ben, that sounds good to me then."

Ben headed back to the alley but most of the people had left. He then went to the doc's office to check on the patient.

Doc looked up and spoke, "He is going to live."

So Ben headed back to the sheriff's office to see what the sheriff wanted him to do.

The sheriff was talking to some of the town people about the shooting. They were worried about all the shooting that was going on. He would catch the killer.

Deputy Morgan spoke up. "Now we know that he killed two people in cold blood."

Joe Luke shrugged. "Ya he did."

"Why is he doing this to us sheriff?" asked the deputy.

"I don't know, Deputy. Maybe he is coming after me I guess."

"I see."

"It's true, Deputy Morgan."

"I don't get it why he is coming after you."

"Maybe he hates me for killing his brother."

Deputy Morgan made a surprised look with his face. "Are you crazy? Why did you kill his brother?"

Joe Luke put both of his hands down. "I was bringing him back to Dodge to stand trial for robbery and he tried to escape and I shot him. I didn't want to but he tried to kill me. I had no choice but to shoot. Deputy let's go have some dinner I haven't eaten since early morning, we can't do much till morning."

Ben Smith Jr. ran into the sheriff's office where the sheriff and the deputy were eating. "The killer has struck again, Sheriff. He shot Billy Jenkins in the horse stable."

"Ben Smith Jr. go get the Doc and we will meet you at the stable."

Doc Smith came into the horse stable.

The sheriff said to Doc, "How is he doing?"

Doc said, "He's hurt pretty bad, we'll take him to my office. I don't think he's going to make it but I will do everything I can."

~ ~ ~

Later Deputy Morgan helped Joe Luke to go up to Doc's office and they asked him if Billy could speak.

Doc Smith shrugged his shoulders. "You can try."

Joe Luke sat on the bed. "Billy Jenkins, who shot you?"

Billy Jenkins said in a raspy voice. "It was Harry Smith Sr. who shot me in the back." His head fell back against the pillow.

Doc put his left two fingers on Billy Jenkins neck. "He is gone."

"Deputy Morgan, what are we going to do now?" asked Ben Smith Jr.

Deputy Morgan spoke, "Nothing."

"He has to be here somewhere." Ben Smith Jr. scratched his head. "Sheriff,"

Joe Luke scratched his head. "Yes, Ben?"

Ben Smith Jr. walked up to Joe Luke. "The killer did it again?"

Joe Luke showed Ben Smith Jr. an excitement on his face. "Really, again!"

"Now he's killed four men, Sheriff."

"Wow, I don't like this killer, Ben."

"What are we going to do now, Sheriff?"

"We are going to sit and wait, Ben."

"For how long though, Sheriff?"

"I am not sure, Ben." Said Joe Luke.

Ben Smith Jr. shrugged his shoulders. "I see. That is messed up, Sheriff."

Joe Luke replied. "I know, Ben."

~·~·~

Ben Smith Jr. lifted his hat up on his head. "I am getting sick of this killer, Sheriff and Deputy."

"Me too, Ben."

Ben Smith Jr. leaned up against the stable wall. "Deputy, we need a plan and fast."

Joe Luke leaned up against the stable wall. "We do need a plan and fast. We could get another posse together."

Deputy Morgan said. "I guess we can and search the town with the new posse."

Chapter 11

Ben came into the horse stable and told the sheriff, "We searched the town and found nothing." Ben Smith Jr. looked at him. "Sheriff Joe Luke, the killer has to be here somewhere."

Joe Luke put all five fingers up on his left hand. "Well that means he has shot five men in cold blood, Ben Smith Jr. Wow, the killer has done enough damage."

"I couldn't agree more, Sheriff."

"Thank you, Ben."

"You are welcome, Sheriff."

"What now, Sheriff?" Asked Ben Smith Jr.

Joe Luke shrugged his shoulders. "Nothing."

Deputy Morgan interrupted Joe Luke and Ben Smith Jr., "Well we still have to find that killer you guys." He shrugged his shoulders.

Ben Smith Jr. jumped up off the hay bail. "Yes, we do. We don't want him to do anymore damage in the town."

Joe Luke spoke, "You are right, Ben."

Ben Smith Jr. spoke back. "I am?"

Joe Luke scratched his head. "Yes, we don't want him to damage the town."

Deputy Morgan scratched his head. "Who is going to be the bait?"

"I am," said Joe Luke.

"Are you crazy?" asked Deputy Morgan.

Ben Smith Jr. made a weird face. "This is crazy, Joe Luke."

Joe Luke shrugged his shoulders. "What's crazy, Ben?"

"You being bait, Joe Luke."

"Well I have to, Ben. The killer wants me."

"I don't want you to, Joe Luke."

"Well I am sorry, Ben. Okay, here goes nothing."

"Okay, Joe Luke. Whatever you say."

"Okay Ben I am going now. If you guys see him, shoot him down."

Ben Smith Jr. saluted. "Yes sir, will do."

The sheriff, deputy, Mac Jenkins Sr., and Ben went out the back door of the stable where they hoped the killer would try to shoot the sheriff. They hoped they would get the killer.

Joe Luke stepped out the back door of the stable on his crutches, gripping his pistol in his right hand. He headed toward the jail to get his rifle.

All of the sudden five shots rang out and Joe Luke was shot in the back. Two hit his back. The third bullet hit Joe Luke's left upper shoulder as he turned his neck to the right. Two more bullets hit Joe Luke's chest. He was shot with five bullets. With each shot he squeezed his trigger and fired off five rounds at the ground.

Joe Luke dropped his six gun and spoke, "I'm shot, I'm shot!"

He stumbled to the jail door, opened it, and fell to the floor with blood coming out of his mouth.

~·~·~

Two more shots that rang out after Joe Luke went down.

Ben Smith Jr.'s brother, Bill Smith Sr., spoke to Deputy Morgan while making eye contact, "I got the killer, Deputy."

Deputy Morgan smiled. "Good job, Bill Smith Sr. Where was the killer at?

Bill Smith Sr. pointed up. "He was on the roof of the stable, Deputy Morgan I shot the killer in the right arm and he fell to the ground to the right of the horse stable."

Bill jumped up in the air. "Yee-Haw!" He threw his hat in the air. "I got the killer!"

Deputy Morgan turned his neck to his right. "It looks like you got him in the right arm, Bill."

Bill Smith Sr. turned his neck to the left. "Yes I did, Deputy Morgan."

Bill and Deputy Morgan picked up the killer and took him to jail.

~ ~ ~

"What is your name, sonny?" asked Deputy Morgan.

"My name is Harry Smith Sr.," replied the killer.

"Really? Do you realize that you killed Joe Luke?" replied Deputy Morgan.

Harry Smith Sr. spoke back. "I did?"

Deputy Morgan made eye contact. "Yep, you did. In cold blood."

Harry Smith Sr. gave Deputy Morgan a surprised look. "That's good for me."

Deputy Morgan scratched his head. "Oh, and why is that, Harry Smith Sr.?"

Harry Smith Sr. shrugged his shoulders. "Because I never liked him and he killed my brother."

Deputy Morgan made a weird face at Harry Smith Sr. "I see." He shrugged his shoulders. "Why did you want to kill Joe Luke, Harry Smith Sr. He was a good man and you're going to hang for his murder."

Harry Smith Sr. clenched his right fist. "He was not a 'good man' to me and I don't care what you think, Deputy Morgan. Joe Luke and I were good friends back in the early days, before he killed my brother. Joe Luke and I worked for a rancher who wanted us to drive some cattle back to his ranch. My brother robbed a stagecoach on the trail to Dodge City and the sheriff rode with the posse that went after him. The sheriff shot him. I swore I would kill him for killing my brother." Harry Smith Sr. spoke to Deputy Morgan. "I might want to have a fair trial and a hanging as well."

Deputy Morgan scratched his head again. "I see."

"Yep."

"Yes, you are right, Harry Smith Sr."

"Well thank you, Deputy."

"You are welcome, Harry Smith Sr."

"I am glad that I killed six men."

"I bet you are happy that you killed six men already."

"Indeed I am, Deputy. Where are you going?"

"I am going to get something to eat at the saloon."

"You might as well bring me back a juicy steak, mashed potatoes, beans, a biscuit, and coffee."

"Okay I will bring you back something to eat."

Harry Smith Sr. winked. "Thank you, Deputy."

Deputy Morgan winked back. "You are welcome, Harry Smith Sr.

～·～·～

Ben Smith Jr. walked up to Deputy Morgan. "What are you doing?"

Deputy Morgan pointed behind him. "I am going across the street to the Long Branch Saloon to get Harry Smith Sr. something to eat right now."

"Okay well have fun, Deputy."

"Thank you, Ben Smith Jr."

"You are welcome, Deputy."

"Ben. Go spread the news that the sheriff has been shot in the back five times with five bullets. And also tell them the killer is named, Harry Smith Sr."

"Okay will do, Deputy Morgan." Ben Smith Jr. saluted.

"Okay sounds like a plan, Ben Smith Jr." Deputy Morgan saluted back. "Okay. And tell them that the funeral is today."

"Okay, Deputy."

"After I get done getting Harry Smith Sr.'s food, I will get the preacher from the church."

"Okay sounds like a plan, Deputy."

"Okay, Ben."

"See you at the funeral, Deputy."

"Okay, Ben. See you then."

Ben gave Deputy Morgan a thumbs up. "Okay bye, Deputy."

Deputy Morgan gave Ben Smith Jr. a thumbs up. "Bye Ben."

～･～･～

Deputy Morgan walked in the Long Branch Saloon.

He walked up and put both hands on the bar. "Sam."

Sam put both hands on the bar. "Yes Deputy."

"Can I have food to go?"

"Sure who is it for?"

Deputy Morgan said, "Harry Smith Sr., the killer.

Sam Jr. gulped. "Harry Smith Sr."

Deputy Morgan rubbed his chin. "Yep that's him alright, Sam."

～･～･～

Mac Jenkins Sr. waved. "Hey, Ben."

Ben Smith Jr. waved back. "Yes, Mac Jenkins Sr.."

Mac Jenkins Sr. spoke, "Let's go talk to these two guys that are coming our way."

Ben Smith Jr. spoke back. "Okay."

Ben Smith Jr. and Mac Jenkins Sr. walked up to Billy Bob and Blondy.

Mac Jenkins Sr. saluted. "Hey, Billy Bob and Blondy Pattan."

Billy Bob saluted. "Hey, Mac Jenkins Sr., how are you?"

Mac Jenkins Sr. waved. "Good." He smiled. "I want you to meet somebody."

Billy Bob made eye contact. "Okay."

"Hey, Ben," said Mac Jenkins Sr..

"Ya?" replied Ben.

Mac Jenkins Sr. put his hand out. "This is Billy Bob and his brother Blondy. Billy Bob and Blondy."

"Yes?" replied the brothers.

Mac Jenkins Sr. moved his hand. "This is Ben Smith Jr."

Billy Bob shook hands with Ben Smith Jr. and grinned. "It is a pleasure to meet you, Ben Smith Jr."

Ben Smith Jr. grinned back. "Same with you Billy Bob and Blondy. Hey, Billy Bob and Blondy."

"Yes, Ben Jr?"

"Are you guys going to the funeral today?"

"I think so, if we don't have anything planned, Ben Smith Jr. Why?"

"Joe Luke is dead."

"What! He's dead?" they gasped.

"Joe Luke has been shot five Times in the back with five bullets."

"Wow I will go let Daisy Owens and Duke Owens know." Said Billy Bob.

"Okay sounds like a plan, Billy Bob. I will get a few people here as well."

"Okay Ben Smith Jr. Sounds like a plan."

"Okay thank you Billy Bob," Ben Smith Jr. said with a salute.

"You are welcome. Let's go do it," said Billy Bob.

"That's right Billy Bob," replied Blondy Pattan.

"Yee-Haw," they chorused.

Mac Jenkins Sr. took his hat off. "Yep. Yee-Haw is right, Billy Bob and Blondy."

Billy Bob took his hat off. "Thank you, Mac Jenkins Sr.."

Blondy Pattan put his hand on Billy Bob's shoulder. "Okay, Billy Bob, let's go tell everyone about the funeral."

Billy Bob put his hand on Blondy's shoulder. "Sounds like a plan, Blondy. Okay let's do it."

"Good thinking, Billy Bob."

"Thank you, Blondy Pattan."

"You are welcome, Billy Bob. Let's go shall we."

"Sure why not, Blondy."

"Okay let's go," said Blondy Pattan.

Billy Bob waved, "Okay see you later Mac Jenkins Sr.."

Mac Jenkins Sr. waved. "See you later, Billy Bob. See you at the funeral."

"Okay, see you there, Mac Jenkins Sr.."

"Okay, Billy Bob."

Billy Bob pointed behind him. "I am going to go to the Dodge House to let Duke Owens and Daisy Owens now, Mac Jenkins Sr.."

Mac Jenkins Sr. saluted. "Okay, Billy Bob. See you later."

~·~·~

Billy Bob and Blondy Pattan walked over the Dodge House where Duke Owens and Daisy Owens were.

Billy Bob went up to the counter, shaking his head. "Hey, Duke Owens."

Duke Owens shook both of their hands at the same time. "Hey, Billy Bob and Blondy. What are you guys doing?"

"Just getting ready for the sheriff's funeral."

"I see."

"Are you coming to the funeral today?"

"Sure why not," Duke Owens said while shrugging his shoulders at Billy Bob and Blondy. "I will be ready here in a second, Billy Bob and Blondy."

"Okay bring your wife, Daisy Owens."

"Okay."

"Okay see you at the Dodge City cemetery."

"Okay sounds like a plan."

"Okay see you then, Duke Owens."

Duke Owens nodded back. "Okay see you two there."

Billy Bob grinned. "Okay sounds good."

~ ~ ~

Billy Bob and Blondy walked outside the Dodge House and spoke to one another as they went.

Billy Bob nodded and patted his brother's shoulder. "Okay, Blondy. We told, Duke Owens."

Blondy nodded back and patted his brother's back. "Yes we did, my brother."

"Let's go let everyone else know that the sheriff has been shot."

"Okay sounds like a plan."

"Okay let's go, Blondy."

"Okay, Billy Bob."

Chapter 12

Back at the jail Deputy Morgan gave Harry Smith Sr. his supper and coffee.

Deputy Morgan handed Harry Smith Sr. his plate. "Here is your steak and mashed potatoes and beans and a biscuit, Harry Smith Sr."

"Thank you, Deputy." Replied Harry Smith Sr. "Wait. Where's my coffee, Deputy Morgan?" he said with a mean look on his face.

"Oh I am sorry, Harry Smith Sr., tin horn." Deputy Morgan gave him a weird look.

"Will you stop calling me that, Deputy?" he said with a mean look on his face. "Everyone is going to call me that."

"You are going to the sheriff's funeral."

"What! Why me."

"Because you shot him in cold blood. Let's go, Harry Smith Sr. It is time for Joe Luke's funeral."

"Fine let me out," Harry Smith Sr. said with a mean look on his face.

"Okay I got my gun out and it is pointing right at you, Harry Smith Sr. I am a ways away from the cell door." Deputy Morgan pointed at Harry Smith Sr. with his six gun. "Get in front of me, Harry Smith Sr."

Harry Smith Sr. replied. "Okay, with his two hands up in the air."

The deputy looked at Harry Smith Sr. "Let's open the door now. If you make one false move you are going to get it in the back, Harry Smith Sr."

Harry Smith Sr. looked back. "What about my supper?" He pointed his thumb back at the cell doors.

Deputy Morgan looked down. "You can have it when you come back from the funeral, Harry Smith Sr."

Harry Smith Sr. yelled. "Okay fine then, Deputy!" He opened the jail door with his right hand.

"Okay let's move," Deputy Morgan said while shoving Harry Smith Sr. out the door with his left hand.

"Okay. You don't have to shove me out the jail door."

"We are almost there."

"Okay thank you for letting me know, Deputy."

"You're welcome, Harry Smith Sr. Okay we are here."

~·~·~

Deputy Morgan and Harry Smith Sr. made it to the Dodge City cemetery.

"Hey, Deputy Morgan," hailed Henry Jones.

Deputy Morgan replied. "Hey, Henry Jones. How are you?"

"I am good," he said while shaking the Deputy's right hand.

"That's good. Hey, Henry Jones."

"Yes Deputy?"

Deputy Morgan put his right hand on Harry Smith Sr.'s left shoulder. "This is my prisoner, Harry Smith Sr. the killer. I called him a tin horn."

"Stop calling me that Deputy," Harry Smith Sr. said while freaking out. He threw his two hands in the air and shook the heck out of them. "I mean it right now." He shook his left fist at Deputy Morgan and Henry Jones.

"Sorry, no can do, Harry Smith Sr. This is our preacher Henry Jones."

Harry Smith Sr. replied and shook the preacher's right hand. "Nice to meet you Mr. Jones."

"Nice to meet you as well," said Henry Jones.

Harry Smith Sr. pointed. "I want you to quit calling me that. I had enough for one day, Deputy."

Henry Jones scratched his arm. "Harry Smith Sr.?"

Harry Smith Sr. scratched his head. "Ya Henry Jones."

"There's no wonder why. You are a tin horn, Harry Smith Sr."

"Stop saying that, Henry Jones."

"Nope. I won't, Harry Smith Sr."

"I don't want anybody to call me a tin horn."

"Oh. Yes they will, Harry Smith Sr."

"I want Deputy Morgan to stop calling me a tin horn."

"Oh is that right?"

"Yep."

"Not happening, Harry Smith Sr."

"I want you to stop calling me that."

Henry Jones got mad. "Nope. End of conversation."

Harry Smith Sr. put his hand out with a mean look on his face. "Fine."

~ ~ ~

Henry Jones taped Deputy Morgan on the shoulder. "Hey, Deputy."

Deputy Morgan turned his neck. "Ya, Mr. Jones.?"

"Look everyone is coming to the funeral." Henry Jones pointed.

Deputy Morgan put his fist up in the air. "Alright!"

Harry Smith Sr. looked. "Oh no, that's not good. I am not happy that everyone is coming." He said with a disgusted look on his face.

Henry Jones put his hands up. "Okay everybody. Let's pray. Except for this tin horn right here."

Harry Smith Sr. put both of his hands on his head. "Hey stop it."

The crowd of people started laughing at Harry Smith Sr. the tin horn. "Ha ha ha ha ha."

"It's not funny everybody."

"Ya it is, Harry Smith Sr."

"No it is not, Bill Smith Sr."

"To me it is."

Duke Owens was laughing his head off like a bore. "Ya, I know right."

Daisy Owens was laughing her head off to. "Ha ha ha ha ha ha ha!"

Henry Jones began. "Dear Heavenly Father. We are here today to ask that you, Lord Jesus Christ, please take really good care of our sheriff. And we don't really care about Harry Smith Sr., the tin horn killer. My Father in the Lord, I hope you send Harry Smith Sr. to be with the devil. My Father, thank you for taking care of our awesome Joe Luke. Lord, thank you so much, our Father in the Lord. All of your people love you, except for Harry Smith Sr. Lord everyone loves Joe Luke, except for this tin horn Harry Smith Sr. Our lord Jesus Christ, in Jesus Christ, your name, Amen!"

"Amen, Lord." Replied Billy Bob and Blondy and everybody else.

~·~·~

Brandi Luke tapped Harry Smith Sr. on the back. "Harry Smith Sr.?"

Harry Smith Sr. turned around. "What?"

"I am Brandi Luke, Joe Luke's wife."

"It's nice to meet you."

Brandi Luke looked at her pretty fingernails and shook his right hand. "Ya whatever." She slugged Harry Smith Sr. in the face with her left fist.

Harry Smith Sr. put his left hand on his face. "Ouch! What was that for?"

Brandi Luke raised her left fist. "That's for shooting my husband in the back. Goodbye, Harry Smith Sr. the tin horn jerk."

Brandi Luke walked away from Harry Smith Sr.

Harry Smith Sr. turned his neck. "How come she is not going to talk to me, Deputy Morgan?"

Deputy Morgan pulled his six gun out of his holster. "Because. The reason why she is not going to talk to you, is because of what you did to her husband. Okay Harry Smith Sr. Let's go back to the jail now."

Harry Smith Sr. made a stupid face. "Okay fine then. That way I can try to have the rest of my supper, Deputy Morgan."

"That's right, Harry Smith Sr. After I put you in jail, I am going to the saloon to celebrate Christmas day. Which is today."

"I don't really care, Deputy Morgan," said Harry Smith Sr. while making a fist at the deputy.

"You should care, Harry Smith Sr."

"Well I don't, Deputy Morgan."

"Okay whatever you say, Harry Smith Sr."

"I do say, Deputy Morgan. I don't believe in Christmas, for what I did to Joe Luke."

"Okay well we are back at the jail now. Open the door with your left hand now."

Harry Smith Sr. made an ugly face at Deputy Morgan. "Okay fine."

"Okay now get in your cell, Harry Smith Sr."

"Fine, Deputy Morgan."

"How is your supper, Harry Smith Sr.?"

"Good and this coffee is day old. Give me fresh coffee!" he said with a mean look on this face

Deputy Morgan gave Harry Smith Sr. a stupid look on his face. "Okay, okay, Harry Smith Sr."

"You know that I don't like you," Harry Smith Sr. said, pointing his index finger in the air.

Deputy Morgan looked down. "I did not know that."

Harry Smith Sr. made a weird face and shook his fist at the deputy. "Well it's true."

Chapter 13

Deputy Morgan raised his hands in the air. "Merry Christmas, everybody."

Ben Smith Jr. shook Deputy Morgan's hand. "Same with you, Deputy Morgan."

Deputy Morgan face lit with excitement. "Thank you, Ben Smith Jr.!"

"You are welcome, Deputy Morgan."

"Here is your marshal badge."

"Alright! Thank you, Deputy Morgan."

"You are welcome."

"I never had a U.S. Marshal badge before, Deputy Morgan."

"Well you do now, Ben Smith Jr."

~ ~ ~

Blonde walked outside the saloon doors. He looked up in the air and pointed. "Look everyone. It's snowing in Dodge City."

Bill Smith Sr. walked out the saloon doors and raised his fist in the air. "Sweet let's go make snow angels, you guys."

Billy Bob lifted his leg in the air. "Let's do it, shall we."

Blondy Pattan lifted his left leg in the air. "We shall indeed."

Billy Bob turned his neck towards Ben Smith Jr. "I have one thing to say."

Marshal Ben Smith Jr. scratched his head. "What, Billy Bob?"

"Yee-Haw!" He said while running though the saloon doors and putting his left fist in the air.

"Really? Is that what you want to say, Billy Bob?"

"Yep."

"Okay. Then I guess I will say, 'Yee-Haw!', then."

"There you go."

"Thank you, Billy Bob."

"You are welcome."

Ben Smith Jr. put his left fist up in the air. "Let's play in the snow."

Billy Bob put both of his hands up in the air. "Yee-Haw! Let it snow, God."

Deputy Morgan walked up to Ben Smith Jr. He made eye contact. "What is today, Ben Smith Jr.?"

Ben Smith Jr. rubbed his chin. "Today is December sixth, eighteen-seventy-six."

"Okay sounds good. Thank you, Ben Smith Jr."

Ben Smith Jr. made eye contact. "You are welcome," he said while patting Deputy Morgan on the back.

~·~·~

Duke Owens and Daisy Owens walked up the saloon steps. Duke Owens walked through the saloon doors. "Merry Christmas, Billy Bob and Blondy." He shook hands with Billy Bob and Blondy.

Billy Bob shook Duke Owen's right hand. "Same you, Duke Owens."

Duke Owens saluted. "Thank you."

Billy Bob saluted back. "You are welcome."

THE END

About the author

Cody Pattan is a thankful son, and he is lazy. He likes the Ninja Turtles. He also likes Star Wars; from the Clone Wars to The Last Jedi. His favorite western actor is Robert Fuller, as Jess Harper, and his other favorite actor is Harrison Ford, as Han Solo. He likes going dancing at the Senior Center every third Saturday with the Rock and Roll Oldies. He also enjoys being a writer and an actor. He's got four Holsteins at his house, Anakin, Max, Sparky, and Number 2. He also enjoys hanging out with his friends.

A note to the Reader

Dear Readers,

Thank you for reading *The Life of Dodge City*. We hope that it made you laugh, made you think, and gave you a sense of enjoyment.

The single greatest act of kindness you can show Mr. Pattan would be to leave a kind and honest review on Amazon, and to share this book with your friends.

We know the book isn't perfect, and that's because Cody isn't perfect, but then again, who is? Though fighting a mild handi-cap Mr. Pattan pursued this project with great enthusiasm and a commitment to make it better, step by step.

Thank you again for reading this book. We hope that you enjoyed reading it as much as we enjoyed writing it, and putting it together.

Respectively & sincerely,
Cody Pattan & Isaiah Silkwood

www.ingramcontent.com/pod-product-compliance
Lightning Source LLC
Chambersburg PA
CBHW021934170626
46807CB00007B/3107